Lunansky, Kim – Author
Paranormal Axis: The Sluagh
1-Youth-fiction, 2-Paranormal-Fiction, 3-Youth-horror, 4-Horror-fiction,
Cover Art & Illustrations: Amy Lunansky

PARANORMAL AXIS...

THE SLUAGH

WRITTEN BY KIM LUNANSKY

ILLUSTRATED BY AMY LUNANSKY

Definition:

Paranormal: not scientifically explainable: Supernatural

Axis – a main line of direction, motion, growth, or extension

Merrieam-Webster.com/dictionary

Dedication

To my family,
Who put up with and even
encourage me in my paranormal
adventures and the never
ending search for answers from
the other side.

Thank you for always pushing
me towards the light in a
world that can sometimes have
way too much darkness to
distract you from your true
journey.

I love you.

Contents

Chapter 1

"Autumn is a cunning muse who steals by degrees my warmth and light. So distracted by her glorious painting of colors, I scarcely realize my losses until the last fiery leaf has fallen to the ground and the final pumpkin shrinks. Autumn departs with a cold kiss, leaving me to suffer the frigid grasp of winter in prolonged nightfall."

-Richelle E. Goodrich

The final days of summer weather were seeping away and starting to turn cooler. There was a promise of soon to be colorful leaves rustling underfoot, back to school routines starting up and early mornings - ugh. I don't mind going back to school so much, it's great to see everyone and catch up on their summer adventures but I am so not a morning person. Waking up and it's still dark outside. Who thinks this stuff up? Why can't school start at lunch time?

I can hear my mom calling me. She waits a few minutes between each call and the silence in between tempts me and calls me back to sleep, but each time her voice gets louder and angrier until it's a full out "GET UP"!!! I grumble a response knowing that I have lost the battle on sleeping in and drag myself upright and then down the hall to the bathroom to get cleaned up. The smell of lavender greets me at the door. Mom likes it; she says it promotes a more relaxed state. I'm more of a fruity air freshener type, so I crack the window open, adjust the hot water and wash my sleepiness away.
After my shower, I pick out my favorite pair of jeans and a purple top, throw my clothes on, brush my teeth, tie up my hair into its half pony tail

half bun and I am down the
stairs in no time to grab a
bite to eat. Mom's running out
the door to work and Dad is
yelling at my brother and
sister to get ready now too. I
grab my cell off the charger
and text Jenna that I'm on my
way. She's my closest friend
and we try to meet each
morning before classes start
and then go in together. I
grab my bag and yell "bye"
over my shoulder and I'm out
the front door and into the
fresh air.

It is a bit crisp this morning, but not too cold, just enough to tell you that fall is approaching and to whisk any of the remaining sleep away. School busses are making their routes and people are rushing around to get to work and school. The street is busy and noisy so I put my headphones in and scroll through my song list. I feel like a bit of Katie Perry to get my first day back mojo on. I push play and blast my way to the end of the street I hit the button at the intersection five times so the light might change faster. My phone buzzes and interrupts the song, it's Jenna - "I see you". I smile and look up and see her across the street. She's saying something and waving frantically at something to my left and so I turn my head just in time to see the bumper of a car slam into me.

It sends me flying into the air. The next thing I remember is that I am standing beside myself watching as people rush to the scene to help. Someone yells to call 911. Jenna is crying and is calling my name and then she calls my house to tell them. She stutters and struggles to speak to tell my Dad what happened.

I don't understand what's happening. I can hear everything and see everything that is going on, but no one can hear me or see me. I'm here, but I'm outside of my body. Am I dead? I can't be dead. This can't be real. Panic starts to nudge its way into my gut. I look around at the chaos that surrounds me. People are yelling and crying and some people are just trying to get a peek out of morbid curiosity. I notice that the ambulance is just arriving. I get lost momentarily in the flashing lights and the noise of the sirens. The police are trying to get people to move back so the paramedics can work on me. My Dad comes running in now too. He's calling me "Emma, Emma – Oh God PLEASE – is she gonna be okay? I'm her

Father." The police are
trying to calm my Dad down and
the paramedics have put me
onto the gurney and are
lifting me into the ambulance.
"Dad I'm here. I don't know
what's happening but I'm here,
I'm okay" I say. But of course
he doesn't hear me. He's
crying and sobbing. Jenna is
throwing up in a nearby bush.

I am totally freaking out, but I give myself a mental smack in the head - FOCUS! I decide to rip myself away from my family and get into the ambulance with my body. I'm afraid to let it out of my sight. This is all wrong. I need to figure out how to get back in. The ambulance roars to life again, sirens blazing, and speeds off to the hospital. One guy is calling in codes to the hospital and the other is keeping pressure on my head where it has cracked open. I can't feel anything. I don't feel any of the pain. It doesn't look good though. There is a lot of blood. I try touching myself, but still nothing. THINK, THINK, THINK! I can't think of what I should do. I can't be dead. Isn't there supposed to be a white light if you are dead? That must be a good sign that I'm going to be fine – right? They will help me. I'll be okay. The panic and fear starts to bite back into my knotting stomach.

Chapter 2

"Maybe before you die, it's your ghosts you see."

-Lauren Oliver, Before I Fall

In no time at all the
ambulance arrives at the
hospital and there is a team
of Nurses and Doctors waiting
for my arrival. They run me
inside and they are all
shouting orders at each other
and working in some kind of
crazy distressed order. So
many people are working on me
at the same time I can't
really see what they are
doing. I try peaking around
them or squeeze in but I just
can't get in close enough to
see what's happening. Machines
start beeping and someone
yells "CLEAR" I see my body
jolt off the bed and the
monitor moves in response and
then goes flat. A needle gets
tossed to the floor and one of
the Nurses yells "SHARPS ON
THE FLOOR." There is a lot of
blood.

I start to panic - how do I get my heart beating again? My Dad is there now and they've escorted him into a "quiet room" to wait while they work on me. It is at that moment that I notice this guy just standing in the room watching me. He looks like he is close to my age. He's not wearing hospital scrubs or a lab coat, just jeans and a t-shirt. He looks like the tall dark and handsome type that you would see out of a teen idol magazine. What the heck? Why is he standing here watching this when my Dad has to sit in some other room? He is obviously not working here or helping in anyway.

He smiles at me and says "Hi I'm Fynn, are you okay?"

It's at this very moment that my anxiety takes a new turn – Oh crap – this is it! He can see me – he's a friggin' angel and I'm dead! "I'm Emma and no, I'm not okay. I need to get back into my body. I'm not ready to die."

He looks at my body on the table as it is jolted again while the Nurses and Doctors keep up their frantic pace trying to save me. Then he grabs my arm and says "common' it's going to be okay, but we have to go. We can't be here."

Just as he is saying this a strange fog swoops into the room. No one else see's this fog except for us. It changes as it's swooping from a foggy grey into a darker almost black fog and even starts to form and shape into a bird – a black raven. He pulls at me and yells "Run – NOW". I start following him hesitantly at first and then I hear this really ear piercing cawing from the bird, not a normal bird noise and I decide maybe Fynn has more experience being dead than I do and I run with him as hard as I can.

He runs out of the hospital
and down the street a couple
of blocks to a church that is
there. We continue running
even though we can't see the
fog or anything anymore, until
we are inside the church. Once
we are through the doors he
slows down to a walk and
points to the other end of the
church. "We're going to the
attic. We'll be less of a
disruption there".

I've never been in this church before, even though I have driven by it many times. It is very old and has a very gothic feel to it, I always wondered what it would be like inside. It has lots of archways and stained glass windows depicting saints, crucifixes and other religious relics and events. It smells of old wood and the organ at the front is huge, it looks like something out of a horror movie. We walk straight down the center aisle, past the organ, and the Alter and where the seats are for the choir. There are a few people sitting or kneeling in the pews but they don't notice us. As we start walking up the stairs I ask "How can we be a disruption? No one even sees us."

Fynn smiles, it is warm and kind and makes me feel like everything is going to be okay. I feel a blush rise to my cheeks. "In my experience, I've learned that in this form we are pure energy", he explains. "When you are in a ghostly form you don't need to eat, but you do need energy to be able to function. If you don't get more energy from somewhere you will fade away and then you really will be dead. Did you ever watch any of those freaky haunted investigation television shows?" I nod in agreement. "Well, they pretty much had it right from what I can tell. We can get our energy from people, animals or anything else that puts off a good amount of energy. But right now we don't want to start making the lights flicker or

anything so the church attic
is a great place to hang out
incognito. There are no people
or energy sources too close up
there, but we are not far
enough away from civilization
in case you need one."
Following Fynn into the attic,
I see that it is used as a
storage area and is full of
boxes, Christmas decorations,
extra chairs, candles and all
sorts of seemingly old junk.
It is obvious that no one
comes up here very often. The
dust is thick and the cobwebs
and spiders are aplenty. Well,
at least I don't have to worry
about being bitten. I take a
seat on a dusty chair with a
wobbly leg. Finn chooses a box
to sit on.
"That was messed up back
there, at the hospital, I say.
What was that in the hospital?
That thing, that noise?"

Fynn takes a deep breath and says "I'm not exactly sure but I have seen other people that get caught in it and they just vanish never to return. It didn't take me long to learn that it's safest to just always be on the look-out for it and try to keep ahead of it. No matter what, you can't let it get near you. Any place that has been blessed seems to be safe from whatever it is. I think it might be some kind of demon or something. I came into the church as a safe place and it has ended up not letting me down. I have been hiding out here for a few weeks. I saw your accident because I was out collecting energy then I saw that you were like me, out of your body. Your accident was pretty intense and I wanted to make sure you were okay and to talk to you, it's been a lonely few weeks for me. I'm not sure how I died I just woke up like this - maybe I died in my sleep or a heart attack or something." Fynn tries to laugh it off, but it's an uncomfortable laugh and doesn't lessen the seriousness of the discussion. "I woke up in the hospital too, but I don't know how I got there and I couldn't find my body at all."

For the next few days Fynn and I stayed in the church attic. He showed me everything he had learned about "the afterlife". He taught me what he had figured out about manipulating the energy, How to move things, how to touch people and how to do just creepy weird stuff, like walking through walls.

It was hard at first. You have to learn how to feel the energy inside you, how to call it forward and direct it. The energy itself feels kind of cool. It's like a wisp of cool air that comes up through you like a spinning tornado and then you just throw it outward at whatever you are trying to move. I guess that is where all the sayings come from about ghosts and cold spots. The living must feel the same thing we do. It's kind of funny Fynn chuckled - "I used to laugh at people that said stuff like that."

Chapter 3

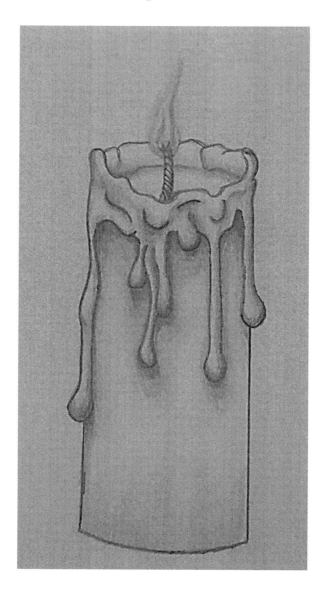

"Doesn't matter who you are or what you believe. Everybody has a ghost story."

-Robin Parrish, Nightmare

I started by practicing on a
small candle that Fynn found
and put out for me. Trying to
concentrate on moving the
candle without touching it is
just as hard as if I were to
do it while I was alive.
Manipulating energy, it seems,
is not something that just
comes naturally. Fynn said he
stumbled across it himself and
he came and stood right in
front of me. He said "pull
the energy into your center
and feel it build there." Then
he took my hand and placed it
on his chest. "Can you feel
that?" I nodded yes. Once I
had a better idea of what I
was trying to feel I was much
more successful. Fynn told me
to pull it out of him and then
push it outward to hit the
candle with it.

Placing both of my hands on his chest I pulled the energy from him and then turned back to the candle and with a mighty mental shove that candle went rocketing from its position on the table. Seeing that candle whipping across the room for the first time was incredible. I couldn't even control the "woohoo" that came out of me in response. Fynn laughed at my ridiculous touch down dance and after a brief "nice work" he said "it is tougher to master moving something just a little bit". So we started working on precision movement skills next. I totally get how babies must feel having to learn everything all from the start – I will never feel the same about baby tantrums again!

We practiced our skills most of the time at night. During the day we went out in search of others like us or any answers or new knowledge we could find about our current state of being. "Huh - maybe this is why people experience ghostly activity at night. Maybe other ghosts work on their skills at night and are out and about during the day too" I said. Fynn laughed. "Makes sense" he said.

Collecting energy was a whole other ball of wax. I felt really guilty about that too because no matter where you take it from you are essentially stealing it. Doesn't matter if you are draining batteries or people, it just isn't yours to start with. Since I was not ready to give up though, on getting back to my family somehow, even if just to send them a message that I'm okay, and it seems that I have no other options if I want to survive I went with Fynn for his Energy Vampire Sucking lesson 101.

We went out just after lunch time and hit a matinee at a theatre close by. Fynn said there are loads of different types of energies in theatres. "Just think about how you felt when you would watch a show when you were alive – depending on the show you can feel tons of different emotions but usually in a strong way, especially if you connect well to the story or characters."

We went in and found a couple of empty spots. We took a seat behind two ladies who seemed really excited to see the show. They were giggling and joking about the characters and what might happen. Fynn instructed me to touch one of the women to feel their energy. I could already feel the bubbling, tickly energy vibrating off her from where I was but I reached over and touched her shoulder. The second I touched her she shivered and I felt myself pulling a flood of bubbly excitement into my body. Fynn pushed my arm off so that I didn't take much from her. I hadn't realized how drained I had been feeling until I received that jolt of energy. It was amazing I felt everything she was feeling and I understood her like she was an old friend. "It's sort of like I can hear her thoughts, I told Fynn. She's superstitious and believes that a ghost just walked over her grave." We both laughed. "That connection is only temporary, it fades pretty quickly" Fynn explained. "Come on let's switch seats – don't want to scare her into the grave!" Fynn joked.

I got up and followed Fynn back out the entrance to theatre. "Can't we stay to watch the show? I wanted to see that one." I asked.

"I was hoping we might find someone who was upset out here." Fynn said. Just as he was saying that a young guy started yelling at this little old man. The little old man had been moving too slowly for him and when he tried to get around him he spilled his drink. Now he was turning purple in the face from screaming at this poor little old man. The old man was trying to apologize and the Manager was running down the hall to see what was happening. Fynn nudged me onwards toward the angry guy. I was a little afraid to touch him because he was so mad. It's just common sense to stay back from people like that but as I got closer to him I could feel the waves of heat and anger pouring off of him in spiky daggers prickling out

towards me. Looking at Fynn
hesitantly and then back to
the man, I reached over and
touched his arm. The same
thing happened as before he
shivered and I felt the rage
he had fill my insides up.
Fynn grabbed me again to pull
me off but this time I turned
fast on him and snapped –
"don't touch me". I could
feel the rage and anger
building and boiling and I
knew I didn't want this energy
inside of me. I looked across
the room and the first thing I
saw was the front doors. A
wall of eight or ten doors at
least, I focused all that rage
on those doors and they all
blew open at the same time.
The wind and leaves started
blowing inside the theatres.
As I continued my focus trying
to drain all of the anger out
of my system I started

slamming the doors – open, closed, open, closed, open, and closed.

Fynn yelled at me through the wind and noise of the chaos to touch the old man. Feeling that extremely rich and overpowering angry energy starting to ebb away I understood now that Finn was trying to show me how different emotions affected your energy.

I looked over at the old man
who was throwing of vibes of
fear and anxiety. The jittery
energy was like sheets of cold
rain pelting at you when you
want shelter. Anticipating the
uncomfortable onslaught of
emotion I reached out and
touched the man's arm.
Instantly my entire body
tightened feeling almost
frozen with fear and wanting
to run and hide. It seemed
like the fear was just as
powerful of an emotion as the
anger was only it gripped me
in a way that I didn't know
how to unleash it. I was so
encased with it I was starting
to get lost in the panic. Fynn
smiled and said "sucks eh?"
Fear and anxiety is the worst
one. I'm not sure how to get
rid of it, but I do know that
love will make you feel better
- come on there's a chic flick

love story in theatre number three. We made our way over to a young couple who seemed to be really into each other, holding hands, kissing and laughing. Although I felt like I was suddenly intruding on their private moments as the invisible third wheel I grabbed onto the arm of the young woman and felt her tender emotions flood through me. Fynn was very right it was like she neutralized the fear and anxiety and left me with a warm glow inside. It was at this moment that I really missed my family.

I wanted to go and see my family and be there to support them or to try and give them messages or something - even if they didn't know I was there but Fynn told me the demons seem to linger around all the places you are likely to show up at. They wait for you. He tried going back to his family and each place he went to try and make contact the fog was there instantly. So, I did not go back yet and mourn with my family, see my funeral or any of those last rites kind of things that give closure to a person. I felt really guilty about that and sad too that I couldn't be there, but I believed Fynn and I knew we couldn't take that risk. I wasn't going to give up though; I would figure it out at some point.

Chapter 4

"What are ghosts if not the hope that love continues beyond our ordinary senses? If ghosts are a delusion, then let me be deluded."

-Amy Tan

I think Fynn knew I was
miserable so the next day he
took me downtown to check
things out. There was an
autumn festival going on and
there were loads of little
booths with people selling
things, some rides and games
as well. The music was loud
and echoing through the area
and everyone was laughing,
playful and excited. You could
feel how the energy was
different, more vibrant. It
was amazing experiencing the
different emotions and
energies of all the people at
the fair. We hit up the kiddie
rides first and went on the
tug boats with some toddlers.
Their joy and excitement was
so pure and intoxicating it
was hard to get off the ride.
I know that's how they felt
because so many of them either
went on the ride over and over

again or had tantrums when their parents pulled them away – which is exactly how I felt. Whoever said kiddie rides are a waste of money and time is WAY OFF! The tilt-a-whirl was fun with a group of teenagers, just spinning and laughing and feeling free to have a good time. Surprisingly even the ferris wheel was fun with an older couple, their feelings shared that it was humbling to be witness to the incredible view at the very top and so appreciative to be relaxing to just enjoy the day with no worries. We spent the next little while like hitch-hikers riding all of the rides for free. We laughed, we screamed, we joked around and we just enjoyed ourselves. It was some much needed relief that had been very long overdue. After we finished with the rides we had a walk around and watched people playing the games. We came upon a little boy who was trying to win a toy. He had to throw these little rings and if the ring landed on the correct bottle he would win a prize. Of course this kid was not aiming at just any prize, he picked the one that was the hardest to get because he wanted the biggest prize. "Oh that's just not right" Fynn said. "Someone needs to tell him the games are fixed." I smiled ear to ear and said "or someone needs to even the odds out." The boy had thrown two out of his three rings already and landed on nothing. As he threw the last one I sent an ever so little helpful nudge in the direction of the ring. It bounced oddly off of the bottle the boy had hit and flew right over to the red winning bottle in the center. The boy started cheering and jumping up and down. The game keeper grumbled that it was a really lucky toss and handed him the giant stuffed animal. I laughed and with a mock toss of a ball, called over to Fynn – "you're up".

Fynn chose a different game.
One where the person has to
climb a rope ladder and it
twists and turns until you
fall off. If you reach the end
you get a prize, but most
people don't because they fall
off. I watched this time as
Fynn flexed his energy around
the ropes to hold it perfectly
still so person after person
was able to climb to the end
and win a prize. The
gamekeeper watched on in shock
and disbelief. After the third
person he decided to shut the
game down and try the ladder
himself to see if it was
sticking or something. I'm not
sure what was funnier watching
the gamekeeper's frustration
with everyone's seemingly
simple wins or watching him go
flying off the ladder. "I
can't remember ever having
this much fun at a fair

before" I said. Fynn was laughing too - "me either". At that, Fynn reached over and slipped his hand into mine. "Is this okay?" He asked. I smiled and nodded my response to him and couldn't help but feel the excited butterflies that were impossibly jumping around in my ghostly tummy.

I hadn't really gotten into the dating scene while I was alive. My parents kept me busy most of the time with different social activities, I was involved in several teams at school, a bowling league on the weekends and then with studying on top, it barely left enough time to hang with my friends never mind getting to know any boys. Sure I knew the guys in my classes and stuff, but that was really where it ended. These new feelings that I was starting to have for Fynn were all foreign and exciting, but I guess that is the way it's supposed to be. I'm not sure though. Even though his hand felt great in mine, I still felt a little lost and confused with everything that was happening.

We had spent most of the afternoon messing with the gamekeepers and because the sun was starting to go down we decided it might be best if we head back to our little church attic. As we were walking through the section with the vendor's tents towards the entrance, one sign jumped out at me. Fortune-Teller, Genevieve Hawethorne. "Fynn – look" I said. "Common' we have to go in there and see if she can see us or hear us – communicate somehow". Fynn looked a bit nervously at the setting sun and finally, albeit skeptically, agreed but said "we need to make this quick".

Inside the tent was a round table with a crystal ball in the center and a stack of tarot cards off to the side. There was a chair on either side of the table. As we entered the psychic was talking to another lady who seemed very excited to be receiving news from the other side. Just as Fynn and I exchanged a curious glance, the psychic looked towards us and said "you will have to wait over there until I'm finished here". Fynn and I both moved over to the corner of the tent she had pointed at, picking our jaws up off the floor along the way. We could hear her apologizing to the lady – "sorry about that dear, spirits just think they can wonder in any time or place they want to. Sometimes you just have to lay down the law and tell them that manners still count in the afterlife. Now, where were we?" She carried on with her prophecies, telling the lady all about her traitorous sister in law and then she was finished the reading. The woman thanked her profusely and took her business card so she could see her again. "Well? She said looking in our direction, common' over here and have a seat, there are extra chairs just pull one up." Fynn and I looked at each other and then Fynn manipulated the extra chair into position beside mine. "Cat got your tongue? What's the problem?" She asked us. "We don't know what we are supposed to do – isn't there supposed to be a light or something?" I asked.

"Give me your hand" the Gypsy replied. I reached across the table to her, Fynn grabbed her other hand and when she grasped my hand I felt the energy connecting us all. Like a swirling tornado surging through us. She really looked the part of a Gypsy. Her long red hair was flowing all around her head and down her back. She wore a rainbow colored hippy dress with a large scarf around her waist. She had huge ear-rings, giant rings on all her fingers and crystals around her neck.

"There is no light for you two yet. You are here to learn. You have much growing left to do" the Gypsy told us. She withdrew her hands and asked us to place our hands on the crystal ball and let the energy flow into it. The crystal ball started to fog up and then we could hear the bird and its sickening caw again. Fynn and I both jumped back ready to bolt if we needed too. "As deep waters hide what lurks beneath from our view, so are many other things hiding right in front of you. The Sluagh (pronounced sloo-ah) are interested you" she said. She tossed a veil over the crystal ball and said "do not be afraid here, I have a friend that I would like you to meet. He will be able to help you on your journey."

She stood up and walked to the back of the tent, opened the flap and rustled through some things. Walking back to us she sat down and wrote on the paper she had just retrieved.

Mike Turner
5273 Girard Street

"He's not too far from here." She handed over the card and I took it. "But what is a Sluagh?" I asked.

The Gypsy said "the Sluagh is a name given to Faerie folk that have gone bad. You see Faeries in general like to play and can be pranksters, some can be very good and kind, but it is said that hundreds of years ago there was a group of Faeries that were just plain wicked. There are many different tales about how they came to be evil, some say they became involved in dark magic, having an interest in becoming more powerful, being able to perform the ultimate tricks and they became addicted to the power and control they could have over others with their horrific behavior. It is believed that they started out working for Witches to learn their skills, but as time passed they felt they were better than the Witches and

betrayed them by calling upon
the Devil himself for his
guidance. The Devil was
entertained by their dark
humor and allowed them to be
his hell hounds for a time and
in turn spared them from the
Witches fury. The Faeries
enjoyed this honor as Hell
Hounds they were able to play
with their prey before
dragging them back to Satan.
For many years they stayed
with him learning his ways and
tormenting those that dared to
wrong their wicked master.
Faeries as a species in
general get bored relatively
quickly and don't stick to
anything for very long and
this held true for this group
as well. Eventually they
became restless and decided
they needed more power. They
decided to try and destroy the
Grim Reaper and steal his

scythe. The Grim Reaper receives all of his power from the scythe; to steal the scythe would destroy the Reaper. Satan was wise to Faeries though, he knew that they would get bored and was waiting for the moment they would try to betray him. The Reaper was one of the Devils oldest friends and although he enjoyed the Hell Hounds, he was not willing to allow the Reaper to be taken by them. The Devil himself had given the Reaper the scythe. When the Hounds were out Satan brought the Witches in for their revenge. Together they created a spell so hideous that to this day people fear even saying the name Sluagh out loud so as not to be mistaken as calling or tempting them to come for you. The Hounds were cursed to become Sluagh forever. They are not allowed to go to heaven of course because they are evil. Satan would not allow them to go to Hell either for their betrayals. The Witches curse also added their own vengeful piece to protect themselves. They proclaimed the Sluagh are never able to set foot on the Earth again. Once the curse had been given the Faeries that had changed into hounds for Satan morphed into a bird – a black Raven. The cawing that can be heard from them is a sickening, horrifying sound. They fly as a group, roaming the earth as birds, not able to take the form of any land creature. They roll in almost as a storm cloud and as they get closer take form into a flock of raven. After being fooled by Satan they became enraged and bitter and it became the goal of the Sluagh to steal the souls of humans before Satan could get to them. Fear of the Sluagh grew among the living and they begin shutting down and locking windows and doors on the west side of their homes to block the Sluagh from being able to enter. It was believed they could only enter your home from the west. Westerly winds were thought to be wicked.

The Sluagh did not let the Witches get away with their spell; as soon as they had the chance they stole the Witches souls and dragged them away in shackles to be used for their bidding. The more souls the Sluagh stole the more powerful they became. The Devil of course was not happy about the Sluagh stealing his souls and a constant battle rages on between them. For many years the Sluagh seemed to have disappeared and so many people just believe it is an urban legend. Most urban legends however, started from a truth and this is no exception. Whatever has kept the Sluagh away for a while is gone now and their interest is in the two of you. Be careful on your journey; travel in the light as they cannot. If they reach you they will drag you away in shackles to forever enslave you in the work of the Sluagh. Some people claim that in between the wretched cawing you can hear the shackles clanging and the cries of the eternally trapped spirits. Go now it's getting late; see Mike because he can teach you so much that will be valuable to your safety and well-being." I thanked her – "we will go see him right away."

After saying our goodbyes, Fynn and I left and made our way, quickly, back to the church. We were both quiet and contemplative the rest of the way back and maybe a bit nervous at being out after dark. The trip back to the church was uneventful. We hung out restlessly once we were inside. Counting the minutes until the sun came up. At the very first hint of daybreak we were on our way to Girard Street to find this Mike Turner.

Chapter 5

"Maybe all the people who say ghosts don't exist are just afraid to admit that they do."

Michael Ende, The Neverending Story

We headed outside and jumped on a bus heading out of town. Kind of nice not having to worry about buying tickets. As we rode the bus through town I watched all of the houses and shops go by. Each one was seasonally decorated for Halloween, drippy looking candles, pumpkins, candies, spider webs and lots of other spooky looking things. It was a chilly day today, drizzly with rain – not that it bothered us at all, but the people on the bus were all bundled up and shaking their umbrellas off as they got on. Everyone had comments to make about the change in the weather and the impending approach of winter. A woman with a little boy was sitting right across from us. He was talking to her about what he wanted to be for Halloween and asking her when they could go and get a costume. He reminded me of my little brother. Last year he was a pirate and my Mom made a lot of his costume – she was very crafty like that. I felt a fresh wave of home sickness and wondered what they were doing right now and if he was going to go trick or treating this year. It would be the first year that I didn't get to participate in Halloween with them. No dressing up, no decorating and no handing out candies.

As if sensing my sadness, or maybe he was just experiencing the same sort of thoughts as me, Fynn asked what was my favorite Halloween and what did I wear? I laughed and said "easy – a few years ago I was Harry Potter. My Mom threw a big themed party and then trick or treating afterwards. Definitely my favorite Halloween memory. How about you?"

Fynn laughed a bit too, "more than a few years ago I was Buzz Light Year. I was so into Toy Story. Everything I owned was Toy Story and of course Buzz was my favorite. I wore that outfit for Halloween and went house to house yelling "to infinity and beyond" forget about trick or treat! I used that costume forever too; I wore it so long the pants were more like capri's before I finally gave them up – haha."

I laughed at that too, just picturing Fynn wearing a Buzz Light year outfit that he had outgrown was an image that I was sure would stay with me for a while!

At the end of the line we hopped off the bus and walked the distance to the house. 5273 Girard street turned out to be an isolated old home on a back road by the Lake. The sign at the bottom of the driveway reads "Colchester Haunted Inn & Spiritual Learning Resort". Fynn and I exchanged a curious look and then we made our way up to the giant wrap around porch. The house itself looks very big from the outside, but is not really well kept. I guess that is sort of standard for haunted houses – why are they all falling apart I wondered? Aren't there any designer ghosts?

The property looks run down and the paint was chipping off the siding. When we get to the front door we knock... mostly to be polite because obviously we could just walk through the door. There is a lot of furniture on the porch, patio sets and wicker chairs, tables, toys and a lot of knick knacks everywhere. "I'm thinking Mike is a hoarder" I sarcastically remark to Fynn.

We hear someone scream and then someone else comes to the door. The enormous thick wooden door creaks and groans as he opens it. How typical, I think. He looks around in a kind of panicked way and says "there's no one here". Then he starts taking pictures of us. His flash is bright and annoying. I see a guy at the back passed this weird guy at the front door and he is waving us in. Fynn goes first and walks right through the crowd that has now gathered to take pictures at the supposedly empty doorway. When he walks through them, some of them gasp and remark that they felt something move through them. More gasping starts and then more rapid camera flashing as I try to follow. The inside of the home looks very old. Everything is wallpapered in some kind of really old floral design. The furniture is really old too with a Victorian feel to it. The piano that is sitting in the living room is so cluttered with pictures that there is no possible way you could even play it. In fact the entire room is cluttered with things. Little ceramic dolls everywhere, they are super creepy. They all look like they are looking at you. There are two young women huddled on the couch. One is crying and the other is trying to comfort her.

We walk into the dining room where the fellow who waved us in is gesturing us to follow him into the next room. The dining room is very dark and heavy. All of the walls are curtained with a thick dark material that is gathered up to make pleats on the wall, once again in a floral pattern. The furniture in here looks Victorian too, the wood table and chairs are all a very dark wood and the china cabinets are filled with more creepy porcelain dolls, old dishes and teapots – lots of teapots. There are no lights on in here just candles and the window blinds and curtains are all drawn tightly shut. This room feels very claustrophobic to me. Like everything is closing in on you and there's nowhere to go. I suppose though, if you are

in the market of providing
haunted inn experiences this
sort of creepy closed in décor
is what your guests are hoping
to find when they get here.
The man that waved us into the
house nods at us to follow him
into the next room. Through
the swinging door I can see
that we are in the kitchen and
it is not at all like the rest
of the house. It is bright and
cheery, and is brand new with
all the latest appliances and
gadgets. It also has a
computer station off to one
corner. "We were sent by this
Gypsy to learn to protect
ourselves from the Sluagh and
to meet with Mike Turner". I
show him her card. "What is
this place?"

"Welcome to the Colchester Haunted Inn & Residence – I'm Mike". The good Gypsy has done well to send you here. You are safe here and you can do no wrong. This is a place where people come to learn and understand more about our universe.

"Great! So I'm dead and my afterlife is to haunt tourists at a creepy Inn" I say. Mike laughs. As far as first impressions go he seems really laid back and easy going. When he laughs, it comes all the way from his belly. It reminds me of Santa Claus only without the beard and red suit.

"You are not dead dear." He says. "You have just transitioned" Mike explains. What humans think of as death is not reality, death is more of a transition. Life is a lot like a butterfly. It starts out as a caterpillar and then transforms into something beautiful and amazing. Everything – all life is a form of energy. You can use this house & its visitors to learn how to use your energy until such time as you are ready to move on again."
Fynn looked at me and then at Mike and said "so those people out there are staying here because they are ghost hunters?"

"Yup, basically" Mike replied. "We don't try to terrorize them though. Each stage of life is about the learning. We hope that people will leave here with enough of an interesting experience that they will reflect on life and dig deeper to find out the truth or more of their own truth at least, others love and joy. No matter what the experience is, there is growth that takes place from that journey. Your soul is, oddly enough, a lot like a video game and it goes to different levels until it finally finishes the game. For example it does level one which could be greed and level two might be wealth and on and on. "I don't really know how many levels there are, except a lot", Mike shrugged. Anyways, some souls are like super gamers and those are the ones who are the most powerful. They pass all the levels of training and then they become hybrid souls. The game of life just keeps going on and on. Does that make sense? We never really die.

You just entered level one of Super Souls versus Sluagh. You gotta just change it up a bit, get used to the new controller and game system, check out the new graphics and powers . Just ride the wave and go with the new groove. The Inn is a great place to experiment and learn how to best utilize your new powers."

Mike types something into his computer and two people come up the back stairs. "This is Mikka and Ray. They are going to show you around and teach you the tricks of the trade." We have a full scale training center here. Mike makes quick introductions and then he is off to speak to the guests, who are examining the orbs in the photos they just took of us.

Mikka is Native Indian. She is very cheery and bubbly and practically bounces all over the place. As she gives us the grand tour of the home she tells us about when she died. She was only 15 and she lived on this property long before the haunted inn was built here. Her family used the lands and the lakes to hunt on and she was injured by an arrow that went astray and hit her by accident. She bled to death from the wound in the area that is now the back porch of the inn. She has been living here since then not knowing where to go. It was not easy to stay here all of that time though. She watched everyone in her tribe grow old. She saw some of them die; none of them left their bodies and stayed with her. Eventually the tribe moved on and left this place and she saw the white man move in and watched the development that happened in the region. She felt drawn to stay on this property and finally when the inn was built she started watching the people coming and going from here and eventually Mike took over and helped her too. She laughs – "I'm not sure what level I'm on but I guess I'm stuck here until I learn something important. I'm good with that though, I like Mike and most of the people that come through here. For the most part it's a pretty entertaining place to be and it's really nice to not be so alone. Friendship goes a long way in eternity. I really missed that over all of those long lonely years."

She seemed friendly enough. It's interesting to see that she has grown with the times. The way she talks and presents herself is very current but she has undertones of a time unknown to me, rich with tradition, culture and meaning from her past. Incredible to think of all the things she has seen and learned in all the time she has been here. As that thought crosses my mind another one follows directly on its' heels – "what if I'm stuck here at this Inn for the next couple hundred years?"

Before I have too long to
ponder that thought I push
those worries aside for now
and decide to pay attention as
Mikka shows us the second
floor which consists of three
bedrooms each with its' own
ensuite and then she brings us
up to the third floor which is
a larger more open space with
2 bedrooms and a shared
kitchenette and living room.
Each of the rooms has their
own theme and they are all
decorated in a masterfully old
world yet haunted creepy sort
of effect. There are old
photos hanging on the walls
that you would swear are
looking at you, mirrors in
just the right places that
make you feel like you need to
look back at to make sure no
one else is looking back at
you or in some cases you are
two scared to look back

because you are sure someone is looking at you. "The continuous dark wallpaper décor and overcrowding of books, porcelain dolls and in general old stuff constantly reminds you that you are not in a normal run of the mill place. It gives the Inn that edge – the haunted creeped out edge" Mikka giggles. As we walk from room to room checking everything out Mikka says "sorry Ray I haven't given you much of a chance to talk. Ray's story is great – tell 'em Ray". Ray smirks, "no worries Mikka, I'm totally used to you stealing the show" he gives her a friendly wink and turns his attention back to Fynn and I. "She thinks it's a great story because she's in it, Ray laughs. I was in my boat on a fishing trip about a year and a half ago, cruising up Lake Huron when a storm moved in. I should have paid more attention to the weather warnings and not gone out in the first place. The boat started to take on too much water, I struggled with it for quite some time before I had to abandon the boat and take my chance to swim ashore. I did it though. It was one hell of a fight swimming through that water to get up to the shore in the storm. The entire time in between the waves and the freezing cold water, even in the middle of summer that water is frigid, when I could spot the shore I could see this woman waving to me to come in and I just kept thinking if I can just make it to the shore I'll be okay, she's there and she'll help me. I did finally make it to the shore and as I got up,

completely exhausted I could
see the woman (Mikka of
course) retreating to a big
house across the way – the inn
– so I dragged myself up to
head toward the house to get
help. I got through the field
and only a few steps from the
front porch when I was struck
by lightning. Killed me on the
spot of course but Mikka came
right back to see if I was
okay. She had been trying her
best to lead me to a safe
place. Turns out my safe place
was with her because we have
been together ever since and
he gave her a kiss on the
cheek. At that moment
lightning strikes outside and
the curious ghost hunters stop
to take notice that there is
not a cloud in the sky. "You
can make lightning?" I ask.
"It's an echo" Ray replies
"like a memory replaying for

everyone to see. It happens every time I think or speak about it. On the anniversary of the date we were able to make the entire thing reply outside - pretty cool...creepy, but cool nonetheless. Mike wasn't much of a fan to my entry into the club though. You should've seen the media attention he got on that - Man struck by lightning in front of Haunted Inn. I guess it made people a bit more nervous to come here. I don't know, I always thought it added a bit more to the authenticity of the place" laughed Ray.

The ghost hunters start setting up video cameras and EVP machines to try and catch more proof on video. The girl that was crying earlier is still very nervous and she seems to seek reassurances from the rest of the team that they can't be hurt or anything while they are there. "These are supposed to be friendly good ghosts – right?" She asks in general to anyone who will answer.

Chapter 6

"Sometimes people graduate but they don't leave. They hang around for years, for no reason. I would think of ghosts like that, I decided."

-Maureen Johnson, The Name of the Star

Ray opens the door to the stairway, leaving the ghost hunters scrambling at the moving door, and says "follow me, this way to the basement". Once we reach the basement I have to do a double take. I was expecting a dingy old concrete room with a musty smell and cobwebs galore. What we walked into was a state of the art room with games that you would typically see at an arcade. Riding games, pinball machines, console games, just about anything you could think up was in there.

"Welcome to the most epic school on the planet" said Ray "The difference with these games from your regular arcade games is these ones are used to enhance ghostly knowledge and abilities."

As you learned your new skills at walking through walls, moving things and manipulating energy for your own use and needs you get higher and higher in the games. Once you get to a certain level in training on the games you graduate so to speak and move on to bigger and better things.

Ray explained that Mike is the gaming wizard expert he knows all the back doors and tricks to skip levels. He also knows that to build enough skill to be able to do well in the higher levels sometimes people have to complete the lower levels first. He has developed video training games to help the super souls learn valuable skills like how to shoot positive energy to hold off demons, or in our case Sluagh, learning and finding your energy weapons and defensive skills like how to hide from them, how to kill them and how not to be killed ourselves.

Ray shows them the first game. It's a pinball machine, only you can't use the buttons. You have to be able to manipulate the energy to move the ball around. Fynn and I took turns playing it. We had a blast, but it was really tricky and took a fair bit of practice to be able to manipulate the ball from bouncing off everything at that speed. You have to almost be ahead of where the ball is going to hit and bounce from next so that you can move it to where it will get the most points. The speed of it was really draining though. Did you know that some pinballs reach a speed of up to 150 mph? Of course, that's the one Mike uses for his training simulator. After several hours of pinball both Fynn and I were absolutely wiped and it was definitely

time to go soak some energy
out of the humans.
~I totally get that now, they
need to be here so we can
recharge, but instead of just
taking from them we give them
a bit of a show so they get
something out of this too - a
bit more of a fair trade
situation ~

As we dragged our groggy butts up the stairs, the ghost hunting group was sitting in the dark in the living room with a spirit box asking random questions and trying to make contact with anyone from the other side. The noise the spirit box made was quite annoying. It sounds like radio fuzz, like when you take the old radio dial and turn it really quick never stopping at one station. You just get that fuzz with incoherent noises from the stations you are skipping over. I can't imagine why anyone would want to crank that racket up and listen to it in a dark room hoping for ghosts to talk to them on it.

Fynn and I went over and each sat down next to one of the people. Fynn slid his arm around the one guy like he was an old buddy. The guy shivered and announced that he just got a cold chill run down his back and that all the hair on his neck is standing up. Another guy with an EMF ran over to measure the electro-magnetic fields around him. Of course the thing went berserk lighting up and beeping like crazy. The one girl started snapping pictures off like crazy and asking the ghost to speak to them through the spirit box. Fynn was happy to play along – "Hello, I am here"

Gasps all around as the words came through the spirit box clear as day in Fynn's own voice. Even Fynn and I were a bit surprised at how well it worked. The girl immediately started asking more questions. "Why are you here? Are you trapped here?"

Fynn looked at me not quite sure how to answer that and then after a moment of thinking he said "Not trapped, learning."

Of course the girl wanted to know what he was learning and how did he die? Again Fynn had that look of puzzlement on his face, a bit unsure of how to respond but he did answer again with "learning the after-life" he didn't give a response to how he died. Tired of being in the hot seat he waved at me to get in on the action. I had been sitting beside one of the young woman and not to be outdone by Fynn's display and to be sure to put on a good show, I decided to sit right down on this woman to make sure the shiver I sent her was more pronounced than Fynn's hair raising one. As I did that the girl gasped and then her head went back, it was like she passed out. Before I knew it I was opening her eyes and breathing her air. I could feel everything, the temperature of the room, the scratchiness of the wool sweater she had on - I never wore wool...too itchy. I could smell the dustiness in the house and even taste the stale gum she was chewing - ewww. After just a moment's reflection I noticed everyone was staring at me including Fynn with a look of either horror or complete disbelief. I realized that I had possessed this girl and they knew it because of the way her body responded when I went into her. I figured I had better say something because why else do ghosts possess people other than to communicate?

I tried to think of something that would not be too scary to the guests, so I looked around the room and said "I'm scared and I miss my Mommy".
The other girls in the room immediately responded with their hands on their hearts, with cooing sounds and motherly love and started slamming me with questions. "What's your name? How did you die? Did you get lost?" They also threw out reassurances like "don't be scared, you're safe here and we'll help you."

At that moment Mikka & Ray dashed into the room and the two of them together reached into this girl and helped to yank me out. The effect on the girl didn't look very pleasant, almost seizure like as she convulsed, while they yanked at me to try to persuade me out of her body. With a bit of work they were successful and they guided me off to go see Mike. I felt disoriented, and it took me a few seconds to realize what had happened. The girl looked okay, her disorientation lasted a few seconds also but she seemed to have no memory of what happened. Her friends were all over her trying to make sure she was okay and telling her what they saw.

As I entered the kitchen Mike was there plugging away on his computer. He stopped to look up at me and said "we don't possess people here, it's not acceptable. It can be dangerous for the person and it's addictive to the spirit as they don't want to leave the living body."

"I'm sorry, I said, I didn't know I could do that. I just meant to one up Fynns' shiver."

"It's okay, Mike said, no real damage done this time, but if it happens again you won't be welcome to stay at the Inn anymore. I'm sure you've seen lots of horror movies on possession, there's one common thread with possession and that is that people go crazy from it. Don't let it happen again."

Chapter 7

"All houses are haunted. All persons are haunted. Throngs of spirits follow us everywhere. We are never alone."

-Barney Sarecky

"I think I'm going to take a walk outside – get some air, I said." It was very late, the wee hours in the morning and out here in the country it was very, very dark. I walked out around the property and just a little way further off the front of the property was the lake. I decided to head in that direction, listening to the waves gently hitting the rocks and the beach. It was a soothing sound that I had always liked. It made me think of summer vacations with my family at the beach, making sand castles, feeling the grainy sand slide between your toes and swimming to keep cool from the summer heat. It made my heart ache for normal again. As I sat down in the sand, Fynn came up behind me. "Are you okay?" He asked.

"I am - it's just a lot to let sink in. I mean everything here, not just the possession thing. Obviously we have a lot to learn still and Mike has a lot he can teach us. I think I'm in for that - hopefully with what I learn I will be able to go back to my family and let them know that I'm okay...communicate with them somehow, be normal again - sort of. I don't know. What do you think about all this?" I lay back on the sand and looked up at the millions of stars and wondered at how many there were up there. It was such a different view from the City. Fynn lay down beside me and rolled onto his side to face me. He ran his fingers through my hair and I felt a magical spark go through me from head to toe. I rolled onto my side and looked back at him, his smile is so amazing, my heart melts a bit more each time he does that. "It's all going to be okay, and we will figure this out together. It's all new to us but we have each other and I won't let anything bad happen to you. I promise I will be right here with you, keeping you safe no matter what – and we will figure out everything that happened and how to communicate with our families. Honestly, I can't think of another person I would rather be in this crazy situation with. Once we figure out all the bumps and hiccups, I can't wait to spend the rest of my eternity with you," Fynn said.

At that moment Fynn leaned in
and kissed me and I sank into
him feeling the softness of
his lips press up against mine
and the sparks igniting into a
warm glow that seemed to
spread through my entire body.
We stayed on the beach
watching the stars until they
changed into the rising sun.
Sometimes we talked about the
shapes the stars made or old
Greek mythological stories we
had heard about and even just
some random thoughts, but some
of the time we just lay in
each other's arms snuggling
under the most magnificent,
romantic blanket of stars in
the universe. I couldn't help
but wonder if this is how love
felt when you are alive, but
then I realized that it
couldn't be the same because
no one that is alive could
have the unbelievable

experiences that we are having and for the first time since this horror story started I felt grateful to be exactly where I was. At this very moment I knew that I would never want to be with anyone other than Fynn. I could feel the spark, the glow, the amazing connection to this other being and I knew this must be something that was written in the stars. It was bigger than just us. We are meant to be together and we are meant to go through this journey together. I wasn't sure what I was supposed to learn or do on this eternal adventure but I was ready to take all of my next steps with Fynn by my side and find out what the future has in store for us.

We spent the next days and weeks spending lots of time in Mike's training school in the basement. He had games for everything. Mike was a really great teacher too. He cheered us on and he offered tips and advice when we got stuck. We talked about the Sluagh too. Mike wasn't really sure why they were after us; apparently that's not really a common thing. He was guessing it had something to do with our skills. He said we were learning and advancing at a much quicker pace than is typical of the average spirit. The property at the Inn is blessed so that nothing bad can come on it but we are definitely going to have to watch our backs and be very careful until we can figure out what they want.

Once we had mastered the pinball levels we were able to control moving things with extreme precision and extraordinary speeds. Then we went on to playing old school video games that everyone grew up with. The trick on these ones was to control things without the controller. Essentially when you play a video game with the controller you are utilizing frequencies that you can't see. For example, you move the controller to the left and the controller sends an invisible message to the machine to move to the left. We had to learn to work with those invisible frequencies with our minds. How to sense and find and manipulate invisible frequencies, quite a skill to have!

I remember playing Mario Bros. and how it took me forever to learn that game and save the princess just to find out she was in a different castle. We had to start all over again from the beginning and once we were able to make the characters move we had to fine tune our skills by saving her from each and every castle again until we were done. By the time Fynn and I were ready to graduate from this skill it was almost Christmas and I was so tired of Mario I would've traded any Math teacher in his place without a second thought.

Chapter 8

"To be haunted is to glimpse a truth that might best be hidden."

James Herbert, Haunted

Mike rewarded us with the chore of decorating the Inn for the holidays with our new found skills. We had to put lights all over the outside of the Inn up on the high peaks and on the porch. It would have been a dreadful job if you had to do it as a human. The ladder work would have been a nightmare and the freezing cold winds and blowing snow would have turned most off the job. However, Fynn and I couldn't feel the cold at all and the heights weren't an issue since we just flexed the energy to send the lights flying all around the house until they were all secured properly. The Inn was pretty isolated but we still decorated it during the middle of the night just to make sure no one saw us - apparently 3:30am is the witching hour

because most people are
sleeping at that time so it's
the best time for us to get
things done without being
noticed.

Fynn and I had a blast
decorating the house. It
looked fantastic once it was
done. We even put lights on a
massive pine tree that stood
on the front property. It was
very Christmassy now. It was
also really cool to be able to
be out in the snow without
being cold. It was like
sitting in the window admiring
the beauty of it, only I was
able to be inside that beauty
and enjoy it without needing
all the winter gear or the
fireplace.

We even flexed our energy on the snow a bit and decided to have a contest. I cleared the driveway and walking path and built a snowman. When I was done, I turned to see that Fynn had built a snow castle. It was amazing! There was even a room inside with an open ceiling so you could look up at the stars. It sparkled and shined under the moonlight like a magical castle from a dream. I looked at it in awe – "it's beautiful" I said.

"Not comparable to the beauty before me. You are so…" Fynn was abruptly cut off by Mike who had come up behind us – "are you insane? Take this castle down – NOW! There aren't any humans running Inns on the planet that can build snow castles like this. Seriously I have to explain this to you? Isn't' this just common knowledge? – the two of you cause me more grief and bend more rules than any other ghosts I know! Why do I put up with this? I should just retire and go someplace nice and warm where there aren't any ghosts bugging me all the time" Mike grumbled all the way back into the Inn.

Mikka and Ray had come out to
see the spectacle and we were
all getting a pretty good
laugh out of it. We destroyed
the castle with an epic
couple's snow battle with snow
balls the size of snow men,
snow tornado's and flying snow
walls. I'm pretty sure Fynn
and I won, but if you were to
ask Mikka and Ray that is
still up for debate. Of course
technically speaking no one
was hit with the snowballs
because they went right
through us so we may just have
to settle with a tie game for
now and have a rematch later.

Training took on a bit of a
lull during Christmas. Mike
had family that was staying at
the Inn that didn't really
want to have any ghostly
experiences so we had to cool
it and instead we Googled
different festivals and
activities that were going on
nearby and decided to go
recharge and have some fun
away from the Inn at those.
There was an ice sculpture
event that we checked out.
That was pretty cool. Fynn and
I vowed that we would have to
have an ice sculpting contest
later back at the Inn. We saw
some carolers, horse drawn
sleigh rides, Christmas tree
lightings and enjoyed looking
in the shops. We had to sneak
out to see the tree lighting
though, Mike thought it was
too dangerous for us to go out
at night. There was a church

right across the street though so we risked it and made it an overnight trip and stayed there until the sun came up the next day. Mike was busy with his family – Mikka and Ray covered for us so he didn't have the chance to notice we were gone.

The people watching was definitely the hardest part for both of us. It again reminded us of our families and how much we missed them, especially at this time of year.

Chapter 9

"Change can be scary, but you know what's scarier? Allowing fear to stop you from growing, evolving and progressing."

Mandy Hale

Once the holidays had passed it was back to the training. Mike had us hooked up with a game to train you on how to show or reveal yourself to people. It covered everything from orbs, zooming orbs, colorful orbs, shadows all the way to complete apparitions. It was set up like a 'wack a mole' game. The type you used to play when you were little, where the mole pops up out of the hole and you have to wack it with a hammer. The more times you wack the higher your score, but the mole moves faster and faster and is hard to catch. The funny part of our game or I guess the incentive for our game was that it was me versus Fynn. We had to take turns being the mole. Once we appeared as an orb or apparition the person playing would try and wack you. Mike had a portal that 'the mole' had to stand on that would put us in the game. Once you were in the game you had to learn to move and portal yourself around as an orb or apparition. The better and faster you got at it the less likely Fynn was to wack me. Of course Fynn got his turn to be the mole too and paybacks were, well – you know.

As Fynn and I got closer to
the mastery level on the wack
a mole game Mike came to find
us. He said that the Gypsy had
called him today and she had
found a young girl that needed
to be brought to the Inn. He
asked if we would mind going
into town and picking her up
and bringing her back. They
were worried if she tried to
make the trip alone she would
get lost. Fynn and I were a
bit surprised that he had
chosen us over Mikka and Ray
to go, but we were up for a
road trip. It had been a few
weeks since we had been away
from training and we were
looking forward to some fun.
Mike told us we needed to meet
her at the hospital, room 402.
It was the same hospital where
I had died.

Fynn and I exchanged a worried glance and just as I was about to say something Mike responded – "Emma I know you came from there and it's a hard memory, but this is a child a lot younger than you and she's there, scared and confused and alone. I need you to be brave and go get her. Just remember that no matter what you see or come across each experience here or there and each transition is about learning, leveling up. It's an easy trip; you can be there and back while the sun is still up."

"Okay I'll do it Mike, we'll tell her she doesn't need to be scared" I said.

At the first crack of light we started the long walk into town to catch the bus back into the City. We were at the end of January now and the countryside was deep in hibernation, everything was covered in a blanket of white. We didn't see very many people in the town at all it seemed that they were all in hibernation too. There were a few people at the bus depot though waiting to get into the City, probably on their way to work. It was a relatively quiet bus ride, people reading the paper and just watching the houses go by. "I'm a bit nervous about this" I admitted to Fynn. "Maybe when we get her from the hospital we could pop by my house? I would love to just see my family again and see that they are okay. I know I'm not ready to communicate with them effectively yet and we'll still come back to the Inn, but do you think it would be okay if we just checked in on them?"

I could tell this was not in Fynn's comfort zone but he still smiled and said "we'll see what we can manage okay?" I nodded and put my head on his shoulder and for the rest of the ride I watched out the window as the cold morning fog lifted and dissipated into a clear sunny but bitterly cold day.

Once we got off the bus it wasn't too far of a walk to the hospital. Not very many people were venturing outside even in the City. Everything was iced over, boots crunched on the frozen snow and the wind howled and pushed with a wicked cold force. I felt lucky that it didn't bother me at all; it didn't take much to remember how much I hated that feeling of cold seeping into your bones though.

As Fynn and I approached the hospital I held Fynn's hand a little bit tighter. He smiled his warm beautiful smile and his fantastic green eyes sparkling against the snowy horizon and he said "common' let's get this over with". We went in through the front revolving doors and the anxious sounds of being in a hospital immediately assaulted our ears. Beeping machines, gurneys with squeaky wheels, Doctors being paged over-head and the worried conversations of the people around us. We saw a sign to go straight for the elevators so we followed our way down the long sterile corridor.

We find the elevator and ride up to the 4th floor. I always hated riding hospital elevators; they make my stomach feel sick the way they move it feels like the bottom drops out…not that I could feel that today. Once the elevator arrives we see the sign welcoming us to the children's ward. This part of the hospital looks different, cheery and colorful. There are lots of pictures of story characters and rainbows and happy children with band aids but it's not a true happy. The underlying truth of sickness and fear with beeping machines and sterile smells still trickle reality onto this floor too. We follow the directions to 402 and turn right; it's the first room on the left. When we enter the room the curtain is drawn so

Fynn clears his throat and says "hello?" A young girl about 8 years old comes through the curtain. She has the most beautiful blue eyes and long golden hair, the likeness of an Angel. "I'm Rose, are you Emma & Fynn" she asks? Fynn and I smile back at her and nod yes.
"Are you here by yourself? How was it safe for you to be here so long by yourself?" Fynn asks.

"The Gypsy was here with me most of the time. We played checkers. She just left a little while before you got here. She said it was safe for me to stay until you got here, but then we would have to go" Rose replied. "Are we going to the special school house now with the fun games room?" Rose asked.

Fynn and I both laughed. "Wait until you see the games in this school. It's the best school I've ever been too" I smiled and gave her a wink. Fynn crouched down so he was at her eye level and asked her if she liked bus rides. She nodded yes and smiled shyly back at him.

"Let's get out of this joint and grab our bus than" Fynn said. He reached out and took Rose's hand in one hand and my hand in the other and the three of us headed back over to the elevators.

We tried to keep things upbeat for Rose by talking about favorite colors and TV shows. We weren't really sure how she had died or what kind of trauma she had been through, however, both of us had been through enough ourselves to know that it could be scary and it must be that much worse for a child. We tried to put on our best entertaining selves and laughed and joked as much as we could.

We exited the elevator and headed back along that depressing corridor on our way back to the hospital entrance. We joked about how hospital hallways look the same as school hallways and we reassured Rose that the school we are going to doesn't look anything like a hospital. We started telling her about our snow castle, as we were passing the Emergency Room though, the doors swung open and someone pushed a patient out on a bed to go for an X-ray. We all stopped for a minute noticing and remembering the chaos and worry inside there. Each of us had a different and unique experience, but all of us having the same end.
"The entrance is just down here I…"

But I didn't get the chance to finish that thought because out of nowhere the fog swooped in around us and then the cawing started, loud and with a vengeance. Fynn snatched Rose up into his arms. She was screaming and started to cry. He tried to grab my arm and run and I could see him screaming at me but it was no use I was trapped inside this haze of birds, I could hear the agonizing cries of the trapped souls and the shackles and the cawing.

Then everything disappeared around me, the fog became so thick, I couldn't see Fynn or Rose. I couldn't see the hospital anymore. It was so loud that it was painful. The pain was overwhelming. I started to crouch down and I grabbed my ears and closed my eyes to shield myself from the sounds and the pain in my head. That's when I woke up.

I opened my eyes screaming out for help to find myself lying in a hospital bed hooked up to all sorts of machines. As I screamed out the machines sparked and exploded around me, alarms were going off everywhere, and my head was still pounding with pain. I heard my Mom yelling for help and Nurses started flooding into the room. My Mom came right over to me, held my hand and sheltered me from the sparking machines and said "its okay Emma you're in the hospital, you had an accident, and everything's going to be okay." With tears streaming down her face she kissed my forehead and told me she loved me.

"We feel free when we escape –
even if it be but from the
frying pan to the fire."

Eric Hoffer

Did you enjoy Kim's writing?
Want more?

Check out her blog and like her on Facebook
for more paranormal action...

www.wordpress.com/klunansky

www.facebook.com/authorklunansky

Coming soon...
August 2016

PARANORMAL AXIS: *RE-ANIMATION*
BOOK 2

After spending months in what Emma thought to be the after-life where she learned to perfect her ghostly skills with a team of spirits in a Haunted Inn dedicated to helping lost souls, Emma is surprised to find out that she was never dead and in the after-life, but actually in a coma. She is reunited with her family but has woken up to a long physical recovery and is taken to a medical facility for treatment.

Strange things start to happen once she arrives at the facility when she realizes that it is the Haunted Inn. Unsure if she's losing her mind from her head injury, or if something paranormal is still going on, Emma finds that the world she left behind is the not the same world she is waking up to.

Now that she's awake she learns that Fynn, the man she fell in love with after her accident and her other friends from the Inn are in grave danger. Time is working against her while she tries to figure out what is going on in this new awareness, how to reach Fynn on the other side and how to save them all from the Sluagh (pronounced sloo-ahh) an evil entity determined to steal and enslave their souls for eternity.

Join Emma as she is re-animated into what we know to be the real world. An unknown paranormal reality awaits that breaks every rule she knows. Enter at your own risk... you never know what can follow you home.

Paranormal Axis: Re-Animation

Book 2

Chapter 1

My vision was a bit blurry at first but as the haze started to clear and I could see that it was my mother with me and that I was in a hospital. I called to her, my voice sounded weak, almost not mine. The nurse was there taking all of my vital signs and the Dr. was on his way into the room. Mom held my hand while they worked on me and checked me over. All of the equipment that had sparked and malfunctioned was turned off and was being removed from the room. The Dr. started asking me questions while he was checking my eyes – "do you know where you are?" I was a bit slow to respond but I did give him the correct response. He turned to my Mom and told her that it was a miracle I was awake and that they were going to keep a close eye on me over the next little bit to assess any damages and help with recovery.

Mom gave me a hug and told me she loved me. She started explaining what had happened. "You were in a car accident, a man hit you with his car on your way to school and then he took off. They haven't found the man he just disappeared." "Jenna?" I squeaked.

"its okay, Mom rubbed my hand, Jenna was there she saw the entire accident, and she's had a really hard time with this. I speak to her parents a lot and they have her in counseling but she's really had a rough year. She'll be so happy to hear that you are awake. We've all been praying for this for so long, she started to cry. Oh – I better call Dad and let him know. She reached over to grab her phone and I listened while she called him up, then she held the phone to my ear so I could hear him tell me how much he loved me and that he was on his way to the hospital right now to see me.

"Mom? You said she had a bad year? How long have I been out?" I asked.

"Well it's not really a full
year, more like a good chunk
of the school year it's
February 29th. That's not what
is important though. You just
need to get better, that's all
we need to focus on right now.
How do you feel honey?"

"My head hurts a bit but
mostly I'm hungry" I answered.
At that the nurse walked in
with a tray of food and
drinks. She told us that they
were arranging for us to be
moved to a different floor and
that they would be moving me
soon. No need for us to stay
in the Coma unit any longer.

I dug into the sandwich and ate it like I had been stranded on a deserted island, not sure why people complain about hospital food it was the best sandwich I could remember eating. Mom went out of the room to make some calls while I was eating, so I took that opportunity to have a better look around the room, I hadn't taken much stock into what was around me up until now. I guess this was like a ward type room, on either side of me there were several beds all with patients in them, all resting quietly. On my left there were two women, to my horror I realized that one was Mikka and the other one was Rose. Just passed them was the door to the room and through the door, across the hall was the nurse's desk. I could see them bustling about and hear

them talking vaguely in the
distance. Now choking on the
rest of the turkey sandwich I
looked to the right side of me
there were three other beds,
with none other than Mike, Ray
and Fynn.

Fynn was in the furthest bed
and as I looked on passed the
third bed three figures
appeared on the other side of
the bed.

They were sort of misty or see through and dark and menacing looking. They were men but they had distorted bird like features - large beak like noses, jet black feathers and a very large wing span. The cheek bones were much more pronounced than ours and were in fact level with the beak nose which made it look like the nose was just an extension of the cheek bones. The chin and eye brows were more prominent as well, with no facial hair and their coloring was off too. They were more of a sickly grey with dark deep bags under the eyes. The eyes themselves just looked like dark pits with no color or sparkle, just big black deep pits.

The more I looked at them the more I begin to realize they were not something from this world. It was obvious who I was meeting.

They hovered near Fynn and laughed at me as I examined them. Then the one in the front snarled "they are all mine now and you will never get them back from me." With that he disintegrated into smoke that whirled through the room and out the window with the sickening caw of none other than the Sluagh.

Through my panic I tried to
get out of the bed and get
over to Fynn. I knocked my
food tray over spilling tea
all over the bed and floor.

As my feet hit the floor I
realized that I had very
minimal strength in my body. I
immediately fell to the floor
and without enough strength to
hold myself upright I started
trying to drag and crawl my
way over to Fynn. With extreme
effort I managed my way to the
edge of his bed and grabbed
his hand.

As I started to call out to him my Mom and the nurse walked back in to move me to the other room. Simultaneously they both saw me on the floor and came running to get me. Both of them asking questions on how I got there and why I was trying to get there and ignoring all of my protests that I needed to save Fynn and the others. I kicked and screamed as much as I could, but it didn't get me anywhere, I was still weak. They were stronger than me and they all thought I was hallucinating or something. Before I knew it a needle had been shoved in my backside and I was losing consciousness again. I called and reached out to Fynn as I was wheeled out of the room and forced back into the dark sleepy abyss that now stretched out before me.

I woke up later strapped to the bed, not sure of how much time had passed. I was in a different room, and through the window I could see that it was night. Off to the corner of the room there was a chair, my Mom was sleeping in a very unnatural and uncomfortable position. I tried to sit up but the straps didn't give me much room for position changes. At my movement my Mom woke up and came over to check on me. I tried telling her what had happened while I was out, how I knew Fynn and the others and about the shadowy figure that threatened them. It was useless though, she just kept saying that none of it had ever happened, it was all hallucinations. She had spoken to the Dr. and he said hallucinations like this were very common with these types of head injuries. That's why you hear of people all of the time who come back from the brink of death and say they went to heaven or met their long dead Uncle Joe or whatever. She said I needed to try and stay calm or they would sedate me again because getting that excited was not good for my recovery. I protested that this was different but it was pointless I wasn't getting anywhere. Frustrated, I lay back down and pretended I was going back to sleep so I could try and figure out what my next move was.

The next morning the Dr. came in to examine me first thing. He spoke to my Mom and I, but mostly my Mom, about how I was stable enough that I didn't need hospital care and that it was time to start rehabilitating me so I could get back onto my feet in no time. My Mom told him about the "hallucinations" and of course he agreed with her and gave me his own spiel about the anatomical ways that the brain works and interprets things.

Absolutely enlightening – whatever happened to the customer is always right?

After the Dr. left breakfast
was delivered, oatmeal,
scrambled eggs and a muffin.
The oatmeal was scary looking
but I ate the rest. When I
finished breakfast a lady came
in to give me a sponge bath. I
tried protesting that as well
but they weren't interested in
my protests. They had to get
me ready because an ambulance
was coming to get me to move
me to the rehabilitation
center. So, instead I had to
lay there and "just let her do
her job" – forget that I
didn't want a stranger doing
that. Once that was over, the
social worker came in to talk
to me about my hallucinations.
The good Dr. thought it might
be helpful to have someone
else to talk to about that and
get it off my chest. At this
point though I had enough and
I refused to talk to him. It

was the only thing left that I
could control with my body -
they could not force me to
talk. The social worker left
his card with Mom and told me
he could understand me not
feeling ready to talk about
things, but when I did, we
could call and set up a visit.
I just rolled my eyes and
looked angrily out the window.
Mom apologized and thanked him
for coming and assured him
that she would be in touch
again. Mom gave me the look
and I knew the lecture was
coming but before she could
get it out they came to take
me to the ambulance to be
transferred. Mom wasn't
allowed to ride with me so she
told me she would meet me
there later. She was going to
go home first and grab some of
my personal items to bring.
Apparently you can wear your

own clothes in rehabilitation instead of these stupid hospital gowns. The ambulance ride was uneventful until they opened the doors and pulled me out to move me inside. I knew exactly where we were… just outside town at a large house surrounded by lots of trees on the lake - the haunted inn.

The sign at the front door read:

Welcome to the Colchester Physical & Mental Wellness Center.

Author Biography

Kim is a wife and mother of three children. She has always been attracted to the paranormal and things that go bump in the night. Bringing together her love of writing and ghostly encounters was a natural next step.

From her own personal experiences and still unanswered curiosities, Kim layers and blurs the lines of reality in heart-pounding adventures from the other side.

Illustrator Biography

Amy is a promising young emerging artist. Practically born with a sketch pad in hand, she has been fine tuning her artistic skills since she was only 2 years old.

Today at age 17, she has a love for drawing, painting, photography, music and animals and has been recognized by her high school for her leadership qualities. As a part of that program she encourages other students to be creative and achieve their goals.

She is anxious to finish high school and continue on to a post secondary education in animation and looks forward to a bright future as an animator.

Made in the USA
Charleston, SC
27 August 2015